I Am A
Truffle Dog

Written by: C.D. Watson

Illustrations by: David Burk

With Thanks To:

Beverly for inspiration, Cherith for determination, Mom for resources, Liz for guidance, SCD for his patience, encouragement and love, and LUCA for his story!

Special acknowledgements to the many Lagotto Romangolo breeders, owners and handlers around the globe. Their dedication and loyalty to "truffle dogs" made this book a reality!

C.D. Watson, Sevierville, Tennessee USA
cdwatson.author@gmail.com

David Burk
www.dburkart.com
david@dburkart.com

My name is Luca.
I am a truffle dog!
My dad said, "Luca, you are special.
You are smart. You are a truffle dog.
You will learn to find rare truffles!"

I will find rare truffles!
I am a truffle dog!

I look and look!
LOOK! I see something shiny.
It must be a rare truffle.
Awesome! I found a rare truffle.
I will take it to my parents.
They will be surprised.
They will be happy!

ross! Luca," said my mom.
Vhere did you find this
sty bottle?" She puts the
ottle in the recycle bin.
ou are a truffle dog. You will
arn to hunt rare truffles-
t gross, nasty bottles."

will hunt rare truffles!
m a truffle dog!

I look and look. I hunt and hunt!
Look! I hunted this! It was hiding.
It was hard to find. It must be a rare truffle.
Cool! I hunted a rare truffle.
I will take it to my parents. They will
be surprised. They will be happy!

"Luca!" My dad said. "Ewww! Where did you find this poor turtle?" He takes the turtle back to the field. "You are a truffle dog. You will learn to smell for rare truffles-not poor turtles."

I will smell for truffles.
I am a truffle dog!

I look and look. I hunt and hunt.
I smell and smell.
Look! I smelled this. It smells wild!
It must be a rare truffle.
Sweet! I smelled a rare truffle.
I will take it to my parents. They will
be surprised. They will be happy!

"LUCA!" My mom screamed
and she ran.
"Disgusting! Luca, where
did you dig up this dead
mouse?" My dad laughs.
"You are a truffle dog.
You will learn to dig up rare
truffles-not dead mice!"
"No more dead mice!" My mom says.

will dig up truffles!
am a truffle dog.

I look and look. I hunt and hunt.
I smell and smell. I dig and dig
Look! I dug this up! It looks valuable
It smells weird. It tastes strange
It must be a truffle. Hooray
I dug up a rare truffle
I will take it to my parents
They will be surprised
They will be happy

"Yuck! Luca, why do you have this stinky, old shoe?" My dad takes the shoe and puts it in the trash. "You are a truffle dog. Tomorrow you will go to school. You will work with a special, truffle dog teacher. If you work hard you will learn to be a great truffle dog."

I am going to school!
I will learn to be a great truffle dog.

"Luca," said my dad. "This is Teacher Jim. Teacher Jim will train you to be a great truffle dog. "
Teacher Jim asks, "Luca, do you know what a truffle is?"
I do not know what a truffle is.
"A truffle is something delicious to eat. Truffles are very rare. It takes a special dog to learn to find truffles," said Teacher Jim.
Teacher Jim shows me a strange looking clump.
"This is a truffle."

"Luca, do you know where
to hunt for truffles?"
I do not know where
to hunt for truffles.
"Truffles grow in the woods.
It takes a smart dog to learn to
hunt for truffles," said Teacher Jim.
Teacher Jim takes me to the woods.

"Luca, do you know what a truffle
smells like?"
I do not know what a truffle smells like.
Teacher Jim holds the truffle by my nose.
"It takes a dog with a great nose
to smell truffles."
"Sniff, sniff, sniff," I smell the truffle.
Ohhh it smells really, really good!

Teacher Jim asks, "Luca, do you know where to dig for the truffles?" I do not know where to dig for the truffles. "Truffles grow under the dirt at the roots of special trees. It takes a dog who will work hard to dig for truffles," said Teacher Jim.

Teacher Jim helps me learn to look
for the trees where truffles grow.

Teacher Jim helps me learn to
hunt around the tree for the
roots where truffles hide.

Teacher Jim helps me learn to smell the ground around the tree roots to find truffles.

Teacher Jim helps me learn to dig very carefully when I smell the truffles to bring them out of the ground.

Teacher Jim helps me learn how to be a **truffle dog!**

Now I know how to search and hunt
and smell and dig. I find lots of truffles.
I take them to my parents and they
put them in a big basket.
They make delicious meals with
the rare truffles.
They are very happy!

My name is Luca.
I went to school,
I worked hard and I learned.
Now, I am a

Great Truffle Dog!

C.D. "Cat" Watson lives and writes in the beautiful Great Smoky Mountains of Eastern Tennessee. *I Am A Truffle Dog* is her first published children's book.

David Burk lives and works in north Texas with his wife and two children. He has done work for many children's publications, including Cobblestone Publishing's *Odyssey™ Magazine*.

To learn more about the Lagotto Romagnolo breed visit The Lagotto Romagnolo Club of America at www.lagottous.com.

CPSIA information can be obtained
at www.ICGtesting.com
Printed in the USA
LVOW01*1231051115

461074LV00003B/4/P